MADELINE's
RESCUE

by LUDWIG BEMELMANS

SCHOLASTIC BOOK SERVICES
NEW YORK · TORONTO · LONDON · AUCKLAND · SYDNEY · TOKYO

ISBN 0-590-08908-0

Copyright 1951, 1953 by Ludwig Bemelmans. This edition is published by Scholastic Book Ser-vices, a division of Scholastic Magazines, Inc., by arrangement with The Viking Press, Inc.

18 17 16 15 14 13 12 11 10 9 8   1 2 3 4 5 6/8

In an old house in Paris that was covered with vines

Lived twelve little girls in two straight lines.

They left the house at half past nine

In two straight lines in rain or shine.

The smallest one was Madeline.

She was not afraid of mice.

She loved winter, snow, and ice.

To the tiger in the zoo

Madeline just said, "Pooh pooh!"

And nobody knew so well

How to frighten Miss Clavel —

Until the day she slipped and fell.

Poor Madeline would now be dead

But for a dog

That kept its head,

And dragged her safe from a watery grave.

"From now on, I hope you will listen to me,

"And here is a cup of camomile tea.

"Good night, little girls — I hope you sleep well."

"Good night, good night, dear Miss Clavel!"

Miss Clavel turned out the light.

After she left there was a fight

About where the dog should sleep that night.

The new pupil was ever
So helpful and clever.

The dog loved biscuits, milk, and beef
And they named it Genevieve.

She could sing and almost talk

And enjoyed the daily walk.

Soon the snow began to fly.

Inside it was warm and dry

And six months passed quickly by.

When the first of May came near
There was nervousness each year.

For on that day there arrived a collection
Of trustees for the annual inspection.

The inspection was most thorough,
Much to everybody's sorrow.

"Tap, tap!" "Whatever can that be?"

"Tap, tap!" "Come out and let me see!

"Dear me, it's a dog! Isn't there a rule

"That says DOGS AREN'T ALLOWED IN SCHOOL?"

"Miss Clavel, get rid of it, please,"

Said the president of the board of trustees.

"Yes, but the children love her so,"

Said Miss Clavel. "Please don't make her go."

"I daresay," said Lord Cucuface.

"I mean — it's a perfect disgrace

"For young ladies to embrace

"This creature of uncertain race!

"Off with you! Go on — run! scat!

"Go away and don't come back!"

Madeline jumped on a chair.

"Lord Cucuface," she cried, "beware!

"Miss Genevieve, noblest dog in France,

"You shall have your VEN-GE-ANCE!"

"It's no use crying or talking.

"Let's get dressed and go out walking.

"The sooner we're ready, the sooner we'll leave—

"The sooner we'll find Miss Genevieve."

They went looking high

and low

And every place a dog might go.

In every place they called her name

But no one answered to the same.

The gendarmes said, "We don't believe
"We've seen a dog like Genevieve."

Hours after they had started
They came back home broken-hearted.

"Oh, Genevieve, where can you be?

"Genevieve, please come back to me."

In the middle of the night

Miss Clavel turned on the light.

And said, "Something is not right."

An old street lamp shed its light
On Miss Genevieve outside.

She was petted, she was fed,

And everybody went to bed.

"Good night, little girls, I hope you sleep well."

"Good night, good night, dear Miss Clavel!"

Miss Clavel turned out the light,

And again there was a fight,

As each little girl cried,

"Genevieve is *mine* tonight!"

For a second time that night
Miss Clavel turned on her light,

And afraid of a disaster,
She ran fast —

And even faster.

"If there's one more fight about Genevieve,

"I'm sorry, but she'll have to leave!"

That was the end of the riot—
Suddenly all was quiet.

For the third time that night
Miss Clavel turned on the light,

And to her surprise she found

That suddenly there was enough hound

THE END .

To go all around.